COLLEEN
AND THE BEAN

All inquiries should be addressed to:
Barron's Educational Series, Inc.
250 Wireless Boulevard
Hauppauge, NY 11788

International Standard Book Number 0-8120-9076-4

Library of Congress Catalog Card Number: 95-15158

Library of Congress Cataloging-in-Publication Data

Foster, Kelli C.
    Colleen and the bean / by Foster & Erickson ; illustrations by
Kerri Gifford.
        p. cm. — (Get ready— get set— read!)
        Summary: A beaver and an opossum find what looks like a bean,
wonder what kind it is, and eventually discover that it is a seed
good for Halloween.
        ISBN 0-8120-9076-4
        (1. Seeds—Fiction. 2. Pumpkin—Fiction. 3. Halloween—Fiction.
4. Beavers—Fiction. 5. Opossums—Fiction. 6. Stories in rhyme.)
I. Erickson, Gina Clegg. II. Gifford, Kerri, ill. III. Title. IV. Series: Erickson,
Gina Clegg. Get ready— get set— read!
PZ8.3.F813Co   1995
(E)—dc20   95-15158
                                                                    CIP
                                                                    AC

PRINTED IN HONG KONG
5678   9927   98765432

GET READY...GET SET...READ!

COLLEEN AND THE BEAN

by
Foster & Erickson

Illustrations by
Kerri Gifford

BARRON'S

"What is this, Dean?"
asked Colleen.

"It looks like a bean,"
said Dean.

"And," added Dean,
" I'm not keen on beans."

"Put it down, Colleen.
It is not clean."

"I've never seen such
a bean," said Colleen.

"Maybe it's an evergreen bean!"

"I hope it is an evergreen. . .

. . . a Christmas tree
tall and lean."

"Dean! Dean! Come and see
what became of my bean."

"Is it an evergreen?"
asked Dean.

"Well," said Colleen,
"it has some green."

"But it is not an evergreen."

"What do you mean?"
asked Dean.

"It is not for Christmas,"
said Colleen.

"It's for Halloween!"

The End

The EAN Word Family

bean
beans
clean
Dean
lean
mean

The EEN Word Family

Colleen
evergreen
green
Halloween
keen

Sight Words

put
come
down
some
tall
maybe
never
Christmas

Dear Parents and Educators:

Welcome to *Get Ready...Get Set...Read!*

We've created these books to introduce children to the magic of reading.

Each story in the series is built around one or two word families. For example, *A Mop for Pop* uses the OP word family. Letters and letter blends are added to OP to form words such as TOP, LOP, and STOP. As you can see, once children are able to read OP, it is a simple task for them to read the entire word family. In addition to word families, we have used a limited number of "sight words." These are words found to occur with high frequency in the books your child will soon be reading. Being able to identify sight words greatly increases reading skill.

You might find the steps outlined on the facing page useful in guiding your work with your beginning reader.

We had great fun creating these books, and great pleasure sharing them with our children. We hope *Get Ready...Get Set...Read!* helps make this first step in reading fun for you and your new reader.

Kelli C. Foster, PhD
Educational Psychologist

Gina Clegg Erickson, MA
Reading Specialist

Guidelines for Using *Get Ready...Get Set...Read!*

Step 1.   Read the story to your child.

Step 2.   Have your child read the Word Family list aloud several times.

Step 3.   Invent new words for the list. Print each new combination for your child to read. Remember, nonsense words can be used (*dat, kat, gat*).

Step 4.   Read the story *with* your child. He or she reads all of the Word Family words; you read the rest.

Step 5.   Have your child read the Sight Word list aloud several times.

Step 6.   Read the story *with* your child again. This time he or she reads the words from both lists; you read the rest.

Step 7.   Your child reads the entire book to you!

There are five sets of books in the

Series. Each set consists of five **FIRST BOOKS**
and two **BRING-IT-ALL-TOGETHER BOOKS**.

SET 1

is the first set your children should read.
The word families are selected from the short vowel sounds:
at, **ed**, **ish** and **im**, **op**, **ug**.

SET 2

provides more practice
with short vowel sounds:
an and **and**, **et**, **ip**, **og**, **ub**.

SET 3

focuses on
long vowel sounds:
ake, **eep**, **ide** and **ine**, **oke** and **ose**, **ue** and **ute**.

SET 4

introduces the idea that the word family sounds
can be spelled two different ways:
ale/ail, **een/ean**, **ight/ite**, **ote/oat**, **oon/une**.

SET 5

acquaints children with word families that
do not follow the rules for long and short vowel sounds:
all, **ound**, **y**, **ow**, **ew**.